TWELVE
COLLECTIONS

Zoran Živković

Twelve Collections
Copyright © 2005 by Zoran Živković

FG-RS0016L2
ISBN: 978-4-908793-18-9

Cover: Youchan Ito, Togoru Art Works

Neoclassic Fleurons font used with permission of
Paulo W–Intellecta Design

Cadmus Press
cadmusmedia.org

TWELVE
COLLECTIONS

Zoran Živković

Translated from the Serbian
by
Alice Copple-Tošić

Cadmus Press
2018

Contents

1. Days

WHEN I ENTERED THE pastry shop, a purple wave swept over me. Almost every surface was in some shade of this color: the wallpaper, curtains, rugs, tablecloths, chair covers. So were the shades on the lighted table lamps. The muted light gave even the air a purple tint.

I squinted and took a look around. Not a single one of the six small round tables with three chairs each was occupied. The pastry chef was standing behind the display counter, wiping a glass with a purple napkin. His apron was inevitably of the same tone as everything else. He seemed more stocky than stout, and a thick, cropped beard and mustache compensated for his shiny bald head.

He smiled and nodded, putting down the glass and napkin.

"Good evening," he said cordially. "Sit wherever you like."

"Good evening," I replied, returning his smile, and took off my hat.

I hesitated a moment, then headed for the table farthest from the door. I put my coat and hat on the coat rack in the corner and sat in the chair next to the wall. The pastry chef hastened to my table with the napkin draped over his arm, smiling all the while.

"What would you like?" he asked solicitously.

"I'd like to have something sweet."

"You're in the right place. We have a fine selection

of pastries." He indicated the menu in the purple cover before me on the table.

I picked it up and opened it. The pages were a somewhat lighter shade of purple, while the words were written in orange. The pastry chef had not overstated the selection. The list of different pastries filled an entire eight pages.

My eyes skimmed the pages, making their way down the list. The farther I went from the beginning, the less familiar were the names. What, for example, could be hiding behind "livid lightning rod", "shambling violin" or "absent-minded bumblebee"? The "enamored water lily" brought a smile to my lips. Items on the fifth page had names that seemed intended to repel those with a sweet tooth. Indeed, who would order a "stinky grater", "putrid acrobat" or "cheerful carcass" without being in the know?

I closed the menu and put it back on the table.

"It's hard to decide with such a selection," I said. "Might you have something to recommend? I would like something special."

The smile that had seemed glued to the pastry chef's face abruptly vanished. I couldn't properly read the look he gave me. It seemed inquisitive and reproving at the same time.

"Special?" he repeated in a voice that had lost its warmth.

"Yes, something out of the ordinary. I like to try new things."

"We have something special, but it's not on the menu."

"It isn't?"

"It isn't. Have you ever tried stuffed monkey?"

If I hadn't just read the menu, this name would certainly have been a surprise. As it was, compared to some of them it seemed rather unassuming.

"I'm afraid I haven't even heard of it."

"Would you like to try it?"

"Is it some kind of cake?" I questioned in return.

"Yes, it is. Cake with a unique flavor. It's made according to a remarkable secret recipe. This is the only place it can be ordered."

"Then why isn't it on the menu?"

"Because of the price."

Now I was the one to eye him inquisitively. "It's that expensive?"

"It depends on how you look at it. For some it is. For others it isn't."

"All right, tell me how much it costs and I'll decide whether it's for me."

The pastry chef sighed, then looked around the empty room as though checking for eavesdroppers on our conversation.

"May I?" He indicated the chair across from me.

"Of course. Please sit down," I said, rising politely in my seat.

The pastry chef sat down and rested his folded hands on the table. He stared at them for several moments, then raised his eyes towards me. When he spoke again, his voice was softer.

"The stuffed monkey is not on the menu because it's not paid for with money."

"What is it paid for with?"

"Days."

"With what?" I asked, even though I'd heard him quite well.

"Days from the past of whoever orders it."

Silence followed.

"Oh, I see," I said at last. "But how can you pay with days from the past?"

"It's possible. The day you use to pay disappears from your memory. It's as though you never lived it. It becomes part of my collection."

"You collect days?"

"Yes. You shouldn't be surprised. Stranger things than the days of other people's lives are collected."

"I'm not surprised, I just didn't know anything about it."

"My collection is already quite large." He turned around and pointed above the display counter. "It's over there."

I had to strain my eyes. If the lighting hadn't been so soft, I might have already noticed the four long rows of vials, one above the other, resembling some sort of frieze extending the whole length of the display counter. There were lots of them, certainly hundreds: deep purple and spherical, with glass stoppers, like fancy perfume bottles.

"That's where you keep the days?"

"Yes. They must be kept tightly closed, in a dark and dry place."

"You don't say."

"Days evaporate instantly if you expose them to the sun. Humidity is also harmful to them. I have to maintain a stable temperature in the pastry shop the whole year round."

"Who would have thought?"

"Quite so. Regrettably, since I don't know anyone else who collects days, there was no one to show me how to maintain such a collection. I had to learn by experience. Many days were lost until I got the hang of it."

"Do you collect any days in particular?"

"No. I'm not choosy. I let the customers decide which day to give me. Some see a good chance to get rid of an unpleasant past and taste an exceptional dessert in return. Everyone has bad days in their lives that they would happily forget. You undoubtedly have such days as well?"

I gave it some thought. "I do."

"Would you give up one of them to try the stuffed monkey?"

Once again several moments passed before I replied. "I would."

The smile returned to the pastry chef's face. "Very well. I'll bring it at once."

He got up and hastened towards the display counter. He went behind it, bent down and briefly disappeared from sight. When he stood up he was holding a purple tray. Carrying it with one hand, he came back to my table.

He put a small purple plate in front of me along with a knife, fork and napkin. The cylindrical cake also looked purple, but that might have been because of the light. The pastry chef sat down, placed the tray at the end of the table, then took from it the last thing he'd brought: an empty vial. He had a bit of trouble removing the glass stopper.

"Think of the day you will pay with before you put the cake in your mouth. As soon as you taste it, the day will disappear. If you don't think of a particular day, one will be removed at random, and it might be one you'd really hate to lose."

I nodded my head, then slowly picked up the knife and fork. I cut a small piece. The inside of the pastry was a different shade of purple. I brought the bite carefully to my mouth.

The pastry chef swiftly closed the vial as soon as I took the fork out of my mouth. He lifted it up towards the table lamp. What he saw inside made his smile broaden.

"Well?" he asked after I had swallowed the first bite.

I took another, larger piece.

"Divine," I mumbled, my mouth full.

Soon there wasn't a crumb on the plate. I picked up the napkin and wiped my mouth.

"I knew you would be delighted. So far not a single person has been anything but pleased."

"I had no idea something that delicious ever existed. Could I have another stuffed monkey?"

"No."

I looked at him in bewilderment. "Why not?"

"It's for your own good. I'm an avid collector, it's true, but I'm not a dishonorable man."

"I don't understand you."

"In order to understand, you need to know something more about the stuffed monkey. It's not an ordinary cake."

I licked my lips. "I agree with you completely."

"Not only in that sense. It creates an addiction."

"Addiction?"

"Yes. The more you eat, the more you want."

"Doesn't everyone with a sweet tooth dream of finding a pastry like that? If you think I'll overdo it, there's no need to worry. I've had a sweet tooth my whole life, even to the point of overindulging, and I'm as fit as a fiddle."

"The stuffed monkey won't harm your health."

"Then how can it be bad for me?"

Before he answered, the pastry chef put the vial in the wide pocket of his apron.

"You would have fewer and fewer days from your past."

"So what? What do I need those days for, anyway?" I laughed. "This way at least they'll be good for something. I will thoroughly enjoy eating my past."

The pastry chef didn't find my witticism amusing. "That wouldn't be very wise," he said in a stern voice.

"It wouldn't?"

"It's not a good idea to be without a past."

"Why not?"

The pastry chef looked at me for a few moments without speaking.

"I told you I didn't have any experience when I began to collect days. I thought, just like you right now, that there was nothing to lose by paying with the past. I let my first customers eat the stuffed monkey to their heart's content, happy to enlarge my collection. Until they started to disappear."

"Disappear?"

"Yes. Gradually. Every new pastry increased the empty space inside them, like they'd become invisible in that spot. The spaces were quite small in the beginning. They went unnoticed. Now you too have one somewhere."

I looked at my hands, then felt my face. "Where?"

"I don't know. It's no use looking for it. You wouldn't even find it under a magnifying glass. That's why there's no harm in trying the stuffed monkey. It hardly leaves a trace. But after just a few pieces the empty space becomes visible and quickly spreads with each new day from the past that is consumed. The first customers hid this from me, fearing that I would refuse to give them the stuffed monkey. And they simply couldn't live without it anymore."

"So what happened?"

"In the end I found out what was happening. The empty spaces became so big that they could no longer be hidden."

"Did you stop giving them the cake?"

"No. It was impossible. They'd become completely addicted. I had to do the exact opposite to keep the whole thing from surfacing. I kept on giving them the stuffed monkey until there was nothing left of them."

"So, that's how you got rid of them?"

"Only partially. They became invisible, but they're still here."

"Here where?"

"In the pastry shop. Even though they're disembodied they are still drawn irresistibly to the stuffed monkey. So they hang around here all the time. It's because of them that everything is purple. For some reason that color does them the most good. That was the least I could do for them."

I looked around the empty room.

"You can't see them, of course. But it's not hard to guess where they are right now. They have all flocked around us. Poor things. Their invisible mouths are certainly watering. You can't imagine how much they envy you."

I pushed the empty plate to the middle of the table.

"Why don't you remove the stuffed monkey from your selection?"

"But it isn't part of the selection."

"You offered it to me."

"You asked for something special."

"I didn't mean something that special."

"You have no reason to be dissatisfied. Both of us, actually, fared well. You tasted an exceptional pastry without any evil consequences, and I added another day to my collection." He patted the pocket of his apron.

I made a vague circular motion with my finger. "What about the empty space?"

"You won't ever notice it. In any case, it will only do you good. It will remind you of the past and how precious it is. You'd been willing to give it up so easily."

I didn't know what to say in response. We sank into silence.

"Would you like to try something less special, from the menu?" said the pastry chef at last. "Even though they can't be compared to the stuffed monkey, they are excellent pastries nonetheless."

"No, thank you," I hastened to reply as I got up. "Perhaps another time. Until then, good-bye."

"Until the next time," said the pastry chef, getting up as well.

As I headed for the door with large strides, putting on my coat as I went, I was struck by the duplicity of this farewell.

2. Fingernails

MR. PROHASKA COLLECTED HIS fingernail clippings. He'd been doing it since the age of eight, when he cut them by himself for the first time. He was so proud of the fact that he'd managed to cut them without his mother's help and without doing himself any harm that he decided to save the ten little sickles as proof of this feat. He'd had to do it in secrecy because his mother certainly wouldn't have let him keep them. He put them in a little plastic bag and stuck a label on it with the date. Letters were still giving him trouble, but at that early age he was already skilled with numbers. He then put the bag in a hidden place.

Approximately two weeks later, when the time came to cut his nails again, he hesitated but a moment before putting the new little sickles in a bag with the date on it. There was no long-term decision behind this; that would only be formed later. He simply felt it was a shame to throw the nails away. It suddenly seemed that doing so would be throwing away part of his body. True, he was no longer physically connected to the nails, but this did nothing to lessen his attachment to them. They might have separated from him, but he could still keep them close by. Sadness filled him at the thought of the many nails his mother had cut off before he turned eight and which were now lost forever.

He continued to collect his nails in an orderly fashion, but the passage of time brought the problem of where to put the little bags. Every year there were twenty-five to thirty more of them. The shoebox where he kept them was not easy to hide; his mother almost found it two or three times. He felt no relief until his early twenties, when he left his parents' home. His fingernail collection at that time contained more than four hundred little bags that filled all of three shoeboxes. That's when he was finally able to put it in order and go through it without the constant fear of being caught doing something unseemly, although he wasn't the slightest bit ashamed of his secret.

He did feel ashamed, however, of keeping something he cared about so much in such an unsuitable place as a shoebox. It seemed like sacrilege to him; he had to find a more dignified repository for his unique collection. Although he still wasn't earning very much money, he nonetheless managed to set aside enough to order five hundred specially fitted cigarette cases. Had he been richer, they certainly would have been made of solid silver, but under the circumstances he had to be satisfied with silver plating. Every cigarette case had a date engraved on the lid and the inside was lined in purple plush with two curved rows, each containing five sickle-shaped indentations.

It took several months to transfer the nails from the little bags to the cigarette cases. It was a tedious and exacting job. He did it with great patience, meticulously, consumed by the constant fear of getting it wrong. It was extremely difficult to ascertain the finger from which each nail had been cut. He finally got the hang of it and then all he needed was a quick touch to place a given sickle accurately in the proper indentation. He proudly considered himself a genuine expert in this type of identification.

The collection was finally lodged in a suitable repository, but one day as he gazed at it with pride an uneasy thought spoiled his pleasure. What if a burglar broke into his apartment? He would certainly head straight for the cigarette cases, particularly since there was nothing else of any value. Perhaps, in his haste, he wouldn't even check what was inside them. Later he would certainly throw away the nails because for him they had no value. This possibility horrified Mr. Prohaska; he had to prevent it at any cost. He rushed to the bank, rented a safe-deposit box and without a moment's notice started transferring the cigarette cases. He felt no relief until the last one was secure.

He went to the bank once a month to deposit two new cigarette cases. He always spent a considerable amount of time in the safe-deposit vault, enjoying the sight of the neatly stacked little cases. It was on one such occasion that an unexpected thought yet again shattered his moment of pleasure. It all started with an innocuous reflection as to whether the safe-deposit box he had rented was large enough to accommodate all his future nails.

Naturally, he could not know how many more nails there would be, but as a good mathematician it was not difficult to calculate that if he lived to the age of eighty-seven and a half years, the safe-deposit box would be filled to the top with cigarette cases. If he were to live longer than that he would have to rent either a larger box or an additional one if there were no larger boxes. This particular problem had a solution. But not the ultimate problem, one that hadn't crossed his mind before and suddenly struck with all its might. What would happen to the collection after his death?

He needed to prepare for this eventuality as soon as possible. True, there was no reason to worry, he was in excellent shape for his age, but disease is not the only cause of death. Various calamities are lying in wait, beyond our control. The worst thing possible would be for him to die a sudden death, before he was able to arrange for the permanent care of his collection. The safe-deposit box would be opened as part of his estate, necessarily divulging his secret.

This had to be prevented by all means. Yes, but how? Perhaps he could rent another safe-deposit box, not under his own name this time, but anonymously, so that his death would not result in its being opened? The box would still be opened at the end of the rental period. All right, then he would rent a box for a very long period. He wasn't quite sure how long that really long period should be—various durations crossed his mind, from one century to an entire millennium—but they told him at the bank that safe-deposit boxes were rented for a maximum of twenty-five years.

This certainly did not seem sufficient to him. He left the bank depressed, and this dismal mood never left him. The situation only worsened when he remembered another undesirable fact that had slipped by unnoticed. The nails on a corpse continue to grow for some time. He couldn't do anything about retrieving the lost fingernails of his childhood, so he simply had to make sure he got these. Should his collection be missing what might be its most important specimens? So, what should he do? He'd be dead and unable to cut his nails in the grave. Whom could he count on to cut them in his place?

Although this problem never left his mind, he couldn't find a solution—until one rainy afternoon when he least expected it. The solution struck him in a moment of profound enlightenment. It was magnificently elegant in its simplicity, like a mathematical formula. He felt like dancing with joy. He refrained, of course, as a man accustomed to well-mannered behavior, although no one would have seen him vent his exultation.

If death was the main obstacle standing in his way, then there was only one way to overcome it, once and for all. Mr. Prohaska firmly decided that he would never die.

3. Autographs

"Good afternoon. Is this seat free?"

I raised my eyes from the newspaper I was reading on the park bench. The diminutive old man who had stopped in front of me took off his hat, revealing a shock of white hair. His thin mustache was also white, and under it stretched a wide smile.

"Yes. You're welcome to take it." I stood up slightly and indicated the empty part of the bench.

"Thank you." The old man sat down on the opposite end and placed his hat in his lap. He was wearing a double-breasted dark blue suit of an old-fashioned cut. The large, purple, slightly askew bow tie around his thin neck seemed ready to flutter off at any moment.

I went back to reading my paper, but not for long.

"Wonderful day," said the old man.

"Wonderful," I concurred, keeping my eyes on the paper to let him know I didn't feel like talking.

But the old man ignored this signal. "It's a real shame to die on such a day as this."

I closed the newspaper and looked at him inquisitively. "Die?"

"Yes. More than eighty people are supposed to die today in this large city."

"How do you know how many people are supposed to die?"

"That's what the statistics say. Around thirty thousand die every year. That's about eighty a day, or one person every eighteen minutes."

"Interesting," I replied and opened the paper again. But I didn't have a chance to continue reading, because the old man spoke again.

"Those are only averages, of course. On some days quite a few more people die than on other days. Can you guess the largest number of people to die on the same day in the last quarter century?"

"No, I can't." I looked at the paper, but didn't read.

"Two hundred and sixteen!"

"That many?" I said in an even voice, turning the page.

"Yes," affirmed the old man brightly. "It was a true pandemic. The day was as beautiful as this one, but that was just an illusion. Weather is able to generate very nasty surprises. Most of those who died were heart patients. Just imagine—not even seven minutes would pass and someone new would die."

"How awful."

"But then there are other days, of course. The sky descends almost to the earth, it rains without letup, the cheeriest people turn sullen and listless, those with a melancholic side fall into deep depression and are on the verge of committing suicide. Even so, almost no one dies. On one such day the number of people who died was a record low—only twenty-six. Just think."

"Unbelievable." I opened the newspaper up very wide and lowered my head a bit so I couldn't see the old man anymore and he couldn't see me.

"People die for a wide variety of reasons," soon came the old man's voice from the other side of my flimsy shelter. "When you read that someone's died of natural causes, that can mean any of a number of diseases. With some of them you'd never think they could be fatal. For example, just last year there were two cases of death from water on the knee. Didn't you hear of them?"

"No, I didn't," I replied crossly.

"And what do you say to death from hair-loss, from bunions or from tennis elbow?"

"Tennis elbow?" I asked in disbelief, peeking at the old man with one eye around the side of the newspaper.

"Yes, believe it or not. A very unusual case. I can tell you the story if you like."

"No, thank you," I hastened to reply, plunging into the newspaper again.

"Lots of deaths aren't natural," continued the old man unrelentingly. "Do you know, for example, the annual average number of people who die in this town just from being struck by lightning?"

I shook my head, although he couldn't see it.

"Five and a half, in spite of the fact that the area is well protected by lightning rods. But that isn't the only affliction that comes from the sky. Infrequently, people die from objects that fall to earth. Most come from the upper floors of buildings or from various aircraft, but there are actual heavenly bodies as well. Almost every year someone dies from a meteorite impact. Did you ever wonder what the chances are of being hit by a cosmic pebble no larger than a pea?"

I didn't reply or make any movement. My nose was pressed against the newspaper, so I couldn't even read.

The old man paid no attention to my silence. "Almost non-existent. The probability of winning the lottery is far greater. Even so, such misfortune does happen."

Silence reigned. My hopes that the old man had abandoned this one-sided conversation were nonetheless in vain.

"Something much larger might fall on your head too. One poor man met his maker under a piano that crashed down from the ninth floor."

I should have pretended I wasn't listening, but curiosity got the better of me. "Piano from the ninth floor?" I asked behind the newspaper.

"Yes, the ninth floor. They were moving it through

the window down to the seventh floor when the cable snapped. This accident at least makes some sense. The man who died was a retired piano tuner. What can you say, though, about a barber who was squashed by an elephant in the middle of the town square?"

I lowered the newspaper and stared at the old man.

"You didn't hear about that one?"

I shook my head.

"A circus was passing through. In order to drum up interest, they decorated the animals with banners and balloons, fitted them with parachutes and dropped them on the town. The rope on the elephant's parachute got tangled and an innocent barber paid the price. The elephant died too, of course."

I couldn't resist saying, "Really?"

The old man disregarded my scorn. "Yes. But there are happier outcomes too. Recently a reckless suicide jumped off an overpass right onto the head of an off-duty fireman who happened to be passing by. The fireman was killed on the spot and the suicide got off with minor injuries."

I closed the newspaper and folded it twice.

"All of that is interesting, but don't you think that on such a lovely day as this there are nicer things to talk about than dying?"

"Yes, there are, but as I said, people die on such days as this too."

That's when it dawned on me.

"Do you . . . feel all right?" It was an awkward way to phrase the question, but I couldn't think of anything else in my alarm.

"I feel great," replied the old man cheerfully. "And I'll feel even better if you give me your autograph."

He reached into the inside pocket of his jacket and took out a purple notebook and a metal pen. He opened it, leafed through it a bit, and then handed it to me along with the pen.

I took them both. The pages of the notebook were purple, too, and the pen appeared heavy.

"My autograph?"

"Yes," said the old man, as though this explained everything.

"Why on earth do you want my autograph? I'm not any kind of celebrity."

"Not yet. But if you were to become one then your autograph, dating from the time before you became famous, would be quite valuable."

I had thought I was more resistant to flattery. As I wrote my name expansively, however, my conscience wasn't pricked the least bit. I gave the notebook and pen back to the old man.

"I just don't see what could make me famous," I said diffidently, wanting to make amends for my lack of modesty. "I'm quite an ordinary man, I don't stand out in any way."

"Don't be like that. Even ordinary men can become famous. Here, take for example the retired piano tuner, the barber and the fireman I just mentioned. They received an unbelievable amount of publicity. They became authentic celebrities."

I looked at him warily. "I wouldn't exactly enjoy becoming famous for having a piano, an elephant or a failed suicide land on my head."

"Naturally, but we are not in a position to choose. These things happen against our will."

"I hope nothing like that happens to me." I smiled. "You won't get much use out of my autograph."

"That's what the others said. But they were wrong."

"What others?"

"The piano tuner, the barber, the fireman and many others. Just see how many autographs I have."

He took the notebook and thumbed through the pages. Dozens of signatures flashed by.

"Whose autographs are those?" I asked in a soft voice.

"People who died when something fell on them. I collected their very last signatures. My collection includes many more fine stories, some even more unusual than these three." He looked at his watch. "Unfortunately, I won't be able to tell you any of them because your time has run out. You have about forty-five seconds."

"Before what?" My voice had gone down almost to a whisper.

The old man stood up and put on his hat. He pointed upwards.

"Something is going to fall on you from up there."

"What?"

"Well, I can't tell you that. All I can say is that you will become very well known. The media will talk for days about the unbelievable accident that befell you. Your signature will be a real jewel in my collection. And now I hope you will forgive me. I must withdraw as soon as possible. It's not advisable to stay in your vicinity. Goodbye."

I looked at him for a moment as he hurried away and then I raised my eyes toward the heavens. The sky was filled with the blueness of a sparkling clear day, without even the trail of a passing airplane. As the seconds dragged slowly by, the impulse flashed through me to rush somewhere out of the way of the unidentified danger. I didn't, though, because it would have been in vain. I'd given my autograph, so there was no avoiding the fame that awaited me.

4. Photographs

Mr. Palivec collected photographs of himself. He'd been doing it since he was thirty-three. That's when he'd bought himself a camera as a birthday present. It was one of the less pretentious cameras in a fancy photography shop, but even so he'd had to save up for it a long time. For this reason, he'd given himself very modest gifts for his previous two birthdays. When he turned thirty-one he'd had to be satisfied with a second-hand book, which he read with pleasure all the same, and one year later he'd given himself a framed watercolor which, after a bit of fixing-up, gave no indication that he'd picked it up at a sale.

He spent a full three and a half months studying the camera's instructions. He'd never been very good with mechanical things, so a great amount of effort was needed. But his innate persistence and diligence helped him master the art of photography. At least in theory. When he finally put the first roll of film in the camera, he already considered himself an experienced photographer. And then an unexpected problem cropped up.

Whose picture should he take? He couldn't just go out into the street, point his camera at a stranger and start snapping away. There was no way of knowing what the reaction might be. He for one wouldn't like to be accosted like that. There might even be a law that prohibited taking pictures without the subject's approval. What about taking pictures without any people in them? He could, for example, take pictures of buildings, empty landscapes or clouds. No, that didn't seem fitting. Photos should show real life and not still life like a watercolor.

Just when he thought he was up against a brick wall, a simple solution came to mind. He would take pictures of himself! Of course! What could be more appropriate? He was undeniably alive, and it was hard to think there was a law prohibiting a person from taking his own picture. After all, if it weren't allowed, why would the instructions have an entire section on how to take your own picture?

He went straight to work. First he chose the prettiest area in his apartment, prettied it up a bit more, and then read the instructions again just in case, even though he already knew them by heart. It took a bit of thought to find a way for the camera to be at the right elevation in the absence of a tripod. He put one chair on top of another, and then added a few books. The assembly wasn't very stable, but if he were careful nothing would go wrong.

He spent a few moments in front of the mirror sprucing himself up, and then finally sat in front of the camera, holding the thin silver wire used to take pictures from a distance. He didn't snap it right away, however. He suddenly realized that the pose he chose would make a big difference. True, he did not intend to show the pictures to anyone, but they would certainly outlive him. Should people get the wrong impression of him some far-off day just because he hadn't positioned himself properly? He went back to the mirror and spent some time trying different facial expressions. In the end he chose something that might be described as dignified and cordial gravity.

As soon as he'd taken the picture a new difficulty arose. He was dying to see it without delay, but that unfortunately wasn't possible. If he were to take the film to be developed it would be a total waste of money. The remaining thirty-five pictures would be wasted. No, all of the roll had to be used before he turned it in to have prints made. He was tempted briefly to sit in front of the camera again and quickly snap the remaining thirty-five shots. What held him back was the sober realization that he did not need so many copies of the same picture. What would they think of him at the photography shop, anyway? They would have to conclude he was an egomaniac.

He pondered at length about what to do. The decision he finally reached wasn't perfect, but nothing better came to mind. He would continue taking pictures of himself, but at one-month intervals. Every fifth of the month he would take a new picture at the exact same time that he'd taken the first one. This plan had an obvious drawback. Three years would have to pass before he finally saw the pictures. An onerous amount of patience would be required.

With regard to the possible criticism that he was egotistical, there were two recourses. Although the photographs would be similar, they wouldn't be the same as if they'd been taken all on the same day. Minor differences were inevitable. People change over time, and three years was not exactly a short period. In addition, he could do something to help make the pictures different. He didn't always have to be in a pose of dignified and cordial gravity. He could be grave and cordially dignified or dignified and gravely cordial.

He didn't sit twiddling his thumbs while the film in the camera steadily filled with his pictures, taken each time in the same place, wearing the same clothes. He had to make due preparations for the photographs before they arrived. They, of course, deserved the best possible album that money could buy. When he saw how much it cost, with leather covers, pages of highly refined cardboard and a gilded spine, he knew at once that his next two birthday presents would have to be quite unpretentious.

For his thirty-fourth he bought himself a phonograph record in a suburban secondhand store. True, he didn't have a record player, but the record had been quite inexpensive, and he was a great admirer of the symphonic orchestra's conductor. His thirty-fifth birthday present came from an even more unassuming place: the flea market. Only a glance was needed to see that the chipped statuette wasn't made of real marble, but one doesn't look a gift horse in the mouth.

He lit up with joy when he finally received the magnificent photo album for his thirty-sixth birthday. He went to the further expense of buying a pair of thin yellow rubber gloves so he wouldn't touch the album with his bare hands. He was quite fastidious about personal hygiene, but regardless of how thoroughly he washed his hands, they could still leave oily traces, something that most certainly had to be avoided.

Soon the need for a new acquisition appeared. He couldn't use just any old thing to write in the album. It had to be a special pen that slid across the cardboard, leaving a thin but distinct line. He bought it for his thirty-seventh birthday, received considerably in advance.

He set about meticulously writing dates above each photograph's place. He had nice handwriting, a bit slanted, but very legible. The album had sixty-nine pages, each one holding four photographs. He spent two full afternoons at work, concentrating solely on not making any mistakes. That would have been a genuine catastrophe.

After he'd brought the work to a successful close, he realized that the album would hold photographs all the way to his fifty-sixth birthday. That was really good. He would have no large expenditures on his hobby for all of two decades. He could save up for a new album and not have to tighten his belt very much. No longer would he have to make do with highly unassuming birthday presents.

Filled with anxiety, at long last he went to the photography shop to pick up the pictures, thirty-six months after he'd taken the first one. The night before, brow knitted with worry, he'd barely slept a wink. What if the pictures didn't turn out? That was possible, the film was already past its expiration date, and he might have done something wrong. He was horrified at the thought that all trace of three years of his life could disappear just like that. As though he'd never lived them.

When he received the envelope full of photographs, he breathed a sigh of relief. Great restraint was needed not to look at them right there in the shop or on the way home. Before he took out the pictures he put on the rubber gloves. Pride filled him as he looked at his dignified, cordial and grave face on the oldest picture, resembling a real self-portrait and not just a photograph.

His excitement rose higher and higher as he made his way through the bunch of pictures, easily recognizing which of the three traits prevailed in his expression. He couldn't decide what gave him greater satisfaction: how he'd turned out on the pictures or his mastery of photography. Not even a small technical imperfection was able to spoil his happiness. For some reason all the pictures had a slightly purple tinge—most likely because the film had been in the camera too long. Well, all right, he consoled himself, there was no need to split hairs.

He put the photographs in the album with care, making sure that each one was in the proper place. The negative helped him in this regard since it presented them in unerring chronological order. Then he took another look at them and even used a magnifying glass. He came to the conclusion that the pictures looked even better in the album, for that was where his dignity, cordiality and gravity were fully manifested.

Looking at the photographs became a well-established ritual—every Saturday afternoon. Periodically he got the urge to open the album more often, but he resisted the temptation. One shouldn't overdo one's pleasures. Then they lose their charm. Once a week was the right measure.

The Saturday rituals became longer and longer because a new set of thirty-six pictures arrived every three years. Although already an experienced photographer, apprehension still filled Mr. Palivec every time he went to pick up the new pictures, and delight took its place as he returned home from the shop. The only shortcoming was the ever-present purple tinge, but he'd become so used to it that its absence would have disconcerted him.

Just when he turned fifty-six, the album was finally filled. Although he'd saved quite enough money in the previous two decades, he didn't have to rush out and buy another album. Three years would pass before the new pictures arrived. He would spend that time enjoying what now seemed like a finally completed work. He imagined a writer felt the same way after finishing his long work on a novel. And not just any novel, but one in which he was the one and only character.

When he opened the album with gloved hands the first Saturday after inserting the last thirty-six pictures, an unpleasant surprise awaited him. The photographs on the first page had partially faded. His face seemed to be disappearing, while the background remained sharp. He flipped through the pages feverishly and discovered that the same thing had happened to the other pictures.

He closed the album, got up from the table and started pacing about the room. He'd already passed by the mirror when something forced him to go back. What he saw in it was the same as on the photographs. Only the contours of his face were discernible, while everything behind him was in sharp focus. He went all the way up to the glass, but his face was still blurry.

He went back to the table and opened the album in the middle. He was not very surprised at the further change. His chest was still on the pictures, but his head now seemed transparent. It had disappeared completely; in its place was the wall behind him. He drew yellow fingers across the photographs as though he could touch this invisibility. He didn't have to go back to the mirror, knowing without looking that if he tried to touch his face, his gloves would plunge into the emptiness above his neck.

He stared blankly ahead for a while, trying to collect his thoughts. A sober look at his new situation was needed. It clearly had many negative aspects. Not everything was black, however. Now he wouldn't have to buy a new photo album. He could spend his savings on something else.

5. Dreams

First I thought I heard the tinkling of the bells I wore as a child on Willow Day. But I was no longer a child. Then it sounded like the bell around the neck of the sheep leading the flock, the bellwether. But I wasn't in a village. Finally, I concluded from the intensity of the ringing that it must be coming from the belfry of a distant church. But in my dream there was no church.

The realization that I was dreaming inevitably woke me up. I couldn't even see the nose on my face in the pitch black, but there was no longer any doubt. The ringing was from the telephone on the bedside table, cutting the soft silence of the night with its persistent, jarring sound.

I stretched out my hand and felt for the switch to the wall lamp above the bedstead, then squinted in the bright light shining down on me. Turning towards the bedside table, I first looked at the clock. Three twenty-seven. Even though the ringing reverberated without letup, I stared at the clock hands for a moment in disbelief. At long last I lifted the receiver.

"Hello," I said hoarsely.

"Good evening." The voice was deep and mature. I had never heard it before. "Please excuse me for calling at this hour, but we must talk without delay."

"Who are you?"

"I am a dream collector."

I should have disconnected the phone before I'd gone to bed. But who would ever suspect that something like this might happen? I had yet to be the victim of twisted minds with nothing better to do than disturb people in the dead of night.

"Such tomfoolery does not befit your age," I said in annoyance and was just about to hang up when his words stopped me.

"Pygmy firefighters."

I was suddenly wide awake. "Excuse me?"

"You were dreaming about pygmy firefighters with purple helmets who were trying to put out a fire that was devouring a huge spider, and what came out of their hoses wasn't water but . . ."

"I know what came out of their hoses," I said, interrupting him curtly. "But how do you know what I was dreaming?"

"What kind of dream collector would I be if I didn't know what people dream? Not only do I know, I also remember them better than the dreamers. That's why I hastened to call before it was too late. In the morning you most likely won't have any memory of what you dreamed."

I was silent for several moments, gathering my thoughts. Before I said another word, I pinched my cheek with my left hand. The pain was real.

"What do you want from me?" I finally asked in a soft voice.

"Your dream."

"My dream?"

"Yes."

"Why do you want my dream?"

"I want to put it in my collection, of course. I collect dreams with purple details. If the pygmies hadn't been wearing helmets that color I wouldn't have bothered you at all."

"What stopped you from taking it without my knowledge, without waking me up? After all, as you said, I would have forgotten it by morning."

"That would be against the rules. You can't put a dream in your collection without the permission of the dreamer."

I did a bit more thinking. "Does that mean I could refuse to give you my permission?"

"Of course. But that wouldn't be in your interest."

"Really? Why not?"

"Because then you wouldn't get the reward."

"Reward?"

"That's right. Dreams aren't given for free. Everything has a price, dreams included."

"I didn't know."

"Not all dreams have the same price, of course. Most of them are actually worthless. No one collects them. You, however, are in luck. Dreams with purple details are among the very rarest, thus they are the most expensive. You could live a life of luxury for years on what I'm going to offer you for your dream about purple firefighters."

The dream collector waited for me to say something in return, but in my confusion I remained silent.

"Perhaps it would be easier for you to accept this," he continued after several moments, "if you imagine it's not about a dream but rather a work of art. The comparison is not at all incongruous. Many people try to create works of art, but only the exceptional few succeed. It's the same thing with dreams. Many people dream, but the number of successful dreams is very small. That's the nature of things. Talent is needed for dreams as well as art, and talented dreamers are a rarity. You are certainly one of them."

"I had no idea," I mumbled.

"That's what usually happens. Talented dreamers don't know they are talented until collectors tell them. I'm proud of the fact that I have discovered some of the most talented. If only you could see my collection. There's not a single dream collector who doesn't envy me. I have a complete gallery of purple dream master-pieces. Your dream will be in excellent company."

"How nice," I said, not very eloquently, but nothing more coherent came to mind at that late hour. "So all I need to do to get the reward is give my permission?"

"Yes. And answer some questions."

"What questions?"

"About yourself. I have to ascertain some facts. Sometimes there is an impediment that prevents a dream from entering a collection."

"Impediment?"

"Yes. We are not like art buyers in this respect. Such verification would be unnecessary if you were, let's say, a painter and I owned a gallery. Your private life wouldn't interest me in the slightest. But dream collectors have to stick to strict rules. Only the dreams of untarnished dreamers can enter a collection. This requirement has caused me to lose several unique specimens. Don't be concerned, I'm almost certain that everything will be fine with you. Shall we begin?"

"Go ahead," I said after a short pause.

"Have you ever killed anyone?"

"Whatever gave you such an idea?" I replied angrily.

"Please don't be offended. The question is by no means directed at you personally. Murderers dream too. Sometimes their dreams are of a much higher quality than those of ordinary people. One of the prettiest dreams I ever saw slipped away just because the elderly dreamer, when he was a young man, had inadvertently caused a traffic accident in which an old woman died, even though she would have died just the same a few years later. But what could I do? Rules are rules. Let's continue. Are you allergic to pollen or goose feathers?"

"No, I'm not."

"Fine. Has any member of your family in the past three generations been treated for a serious mental disorder?"

I bristled once again but all I did was say through clenched teeth, "Of course not."

"Very good. Have you ever had a contagious disease?"

I thought for a moment. "Scarlet fever and mumps."

"That's all? You haven't had typhoid fever, malaria, cholera, smallpox or the plague?"

I shook my head vigorously, although it was pointless. "No, I haven't."

"Wonderful. Do you take pleasure in torturing household pets?"

"I don't have any pets in my house."

"So, you don't take any pleasure. All right. Are you color blind?"

"How could I dream of pygmy firefighters with purple helmets if I were color blind?"

"That wouldn't stand in your way. You might not know it, but the dreams of the color blind are a real explosion of color. It's a shame that the rules won't let us include them in our collections. Are you afraid of heights?"

"A little," I said reluctantly.

"When you are on the edge of a cliff, do you become totally paralyzed, overcome by dizziness, and covered in cold sweat?"

"I stay away from the edges of cliffs."

"Smart thinking. That means we can conclude that you do not suffer from acute fear of heights. Do you collect stamps?"

"No."

"That's really good. Up until now I've lost the most dreams because the dreamers turned out to be philatelists."

"What's wrong with being a philatelist?"

"There's nothing wrong, of course. I personally have nothing against philatelists; I actually like them, even though they've caused me losses. But those are the rules and I wasn't the one who made them. In any case, you're making great progress. We only have three questions left. Did you ever go through an earthquake stronger than six and a half on the Richter scale?"

"I've never gone through an earthquake."

"Not even a tiny one?"

"Not even a tiny one."

"You're lucky. Even little earthquakes are quite unpleasant. Do you count the steps when climbing upstairs?"

"No. And I usually take the elevator to go up."

"That's not very healthy. It's been shown that people who prefer to take the stairs instead of the elevator live an average of three years, four months and seven days longer. On the other hand, it's hard to say no to comfort. And finally, here is the last question. Did you drink an alcoholic beverage before you went to bed last night?"

I hesitated briefly. "Yes, I did. Half a glass of wine, just like I do every evening."

"Red or white?"

"Red."

Silence reigned on the other end of the line.

I waited a bit and then asked, "That's not good?"

The dream collector sighed noisily before he answered. "No, it isn't. The rules are explicit. Not a drop of red wine is allowed. It counts as strong doping, unlike white wine, which is allowed in moderate amounts. Dreams under the influence of red wine are considered to be artificial, not natural."

"If I'd known, I wouldn't have touched it."

"If you hadn't, it's questionable whether you would have dreamed about pygmy firefighters with purple helmets."

"What now?" I said after a brief silence.

"Nothing, I'm afraid. We're both losing out. You won't get your lavish reward and I've forfeited an excellent dream. But don't lose hope. As I said before, you are a talented dreamer. Just avoid red wine before you go to bed. I'll keep a sharp eye on your dreams. I'll call you again as soon as a purple one appears, although quite some time might pass until the next one. But at least we won't have to go through the questions again. Now, go back to sleep. Good night."

"Good night," I said, after the line was already dead.

I hung up the receiver and turned off the wall lamp. I lay there staring into the impenetrable darkness surrounding me until the sound of ringing came from the distance. The thunderous church bell came first, followed a bit later by the muffled sound of the bell-wether, which quickly segued into the soft tinkling of the bells from my childhood. Finally there was nothing around me but silence.

6. Words

MR. PLUSHAL COLLECTED WORDS. He'd been doing this since the age of fifty-six, after reading his first anthology of love poems. It had been a small paperback with a beautiful purple flower on the cover, although the smell emanating from the book was wholly incompatible with this image. The copy had the stale, musty odor that inevitably permeates books after they spend a long time in a basement secondhand bookstore.

Mr. Plushal might not have bought the anthology. Although he periodically made the rounds of the bookstores, he rarely bought any books, and when he did they were of a quite different sort. He had a small library in his house consisting primarily of handbooks. On raising houseplants, for example. He himself didn't have any plants, but he considered himself very knowledgeable on the subject. Or on cats. He didn't have a cat because he was allergic to their fur, but if anyone were to ask him, he had plenty of useful advice to offer. There was also a handbook on freezer maintenance and repair. True, he had no need for a freezer, but useful knowledge is nothing to be sneezed at.

He had decided to buy the anthology because of the flower on the cover. As a plant expert he knew that such a flower did not exist, but that was the very reason it had appealed to him. He took the book to the cashier in a somewhat uneasy state. It seemed somehow unfitting for a man his age to show an interest in romantic verse. It was almost like buying a pornographic magazine. Luckily the salesgirl didn't take note of the title. All she did was look at the price and take the exact change he handed her.

He knew a thing or two about love, of course. Not from personal experience in this case, either, but was that necessary? Most likely people are born with such awareness. How else could it be? Nonetheless, when he set to reading the book, the unease from the store returned, despite the fact that he was alone. He even blushed. He only found relief with the thought that the anthology should be considered a handbook on love. Then everything became easier and quite pleasant.

He was surprised to find that the words in the book charmed him even more than the tender and exalted feelings. He suddenly became aware of something that had escaped his notice. Beautiful words exist. They weren't necessarily special or rare, rather ordinary words that were to be found in other books too. But for some reason or other they had never looked beautiful in the handbooks. Or rather, their beauty hadn't caught his eye.

The more he read, the more he was filled with the fear of losing something. When he turned a page, the words that stayed behind seemed to pale and evaporate. New ones came to take their place, but this was insufficient consolation. He had to save the earlier ones somehow. It made no sense to allow them to disappear. He could have gone back to them, of course, but then he would never finish reading the book. No, he had to find a better solution. And then he had a flash of inspiration.

He bought a large lined notebook with a leather cover. Nothing less magnificent would suffice as a repository for beautiful words. How could he write them in an ordinary notebook? That would have been almost sacrilegious. He returned to the beginning of the anthology, holding the open notebook in front of him.

Whenever he came across a beautiful word, he wrote it down promptly with his fountain pen. It was not made of gold, in actual fact, but it's hard to arrange everything to perfection.

His handwriting was neat. Not ornate but measured, even a little austere. Beautiful in its own way. Just what was needed to write down beautiful words, not overshadowing them yet consonant with them. He normally wrote with large letters, but for this occasion he made the letters smaller. Just in case. He didn't know how many beautiful words he would find. The notebook was quite thick, but he had to proceed with care.

It was not until he had written down all the beautiful words in the anthology that he mustered the courage to check the results. Would they remain beautiful in his notebook or would their beauty be lost, as in the handbooks? Holding the notebook a short distance away, he breathed a sigh of relief as he took in the four densely filled pages. Not only was their beauty intact, it seemed somehow enhanced. This was probably due to the fact that only beautiful words were present, not those other ones that were not exactly ugly, but did not stand out in any way. The notebook was concentrated beauty.

After he had finished the anthology, he wondered what to do next. The notebook was nowhere near to being filled, it had barely been touched. Could he leave it like that? It would be as if he'd merely chipped off a bit of beauty. No, he had to continue. There had to be many more beautiful words. They all deserved to be in one place. But where should he look for them?

What first crossed his mind, naturally, was another anthology of love poems. He couldn't go wrong there. He'd seen for himself that beautiful words find great expression in love poems. But if he kept buying just this type of book he would soon become conspicuous. Two or three more could pass unnoticed, but three hundred and thirty-five, the number he'd seen in the Main Library catalogue, would certainly give rise to derision. No, he would have to think of something else. And then he had a second inspirational flash.

Who said beautiful words could only be found in anthologies of love poems? They certainly had to be in other books too. Why not even in handbooks? He was already expert enough to grasp a great truth. Beautiful words are everywhere. The skill lay not in the choice of books but in detecting the words. You had to have an eye for them. And he suspected he already had one. There was a simple way to verify this. He grabbed the first handbook within his reach and opened it. The same moment he was blinded by a blaze of beautiful words, as though someone had highlighted them with a bright marker.

He was barely able to resist the temptation to open his notebook and start writing them down. What stopped him was his prudence, something that made him rightfully proud. One couldn't be so impulsive. Where would that lead one? Confusion would reign in an instant. He had to be steadfast and systematic. After thoroughly considering the circumstances, the solution presented itself at last, once again in the form of an inspiration.

He struggled briefly with the thought of tearing up the first four pages in the notebook so he could start over again. But he dropped the idea. Such an important undertaking could not begin in a disfigured notebook. He would have to buy a new one. That alone would be fitting. He chose the largest one he could find. It had a feature that he found particularly expedient: a gilded ribbon to mark the place where you had stopped reading or writing.

The enormous dictionary had sixteen heavy tomes. When he opened the first one, a bevy of sparkling, beautiful words met his eye. The magnitude of what lay ahead did not frighten him, however. He was perfectly prepared for it. Nor could he expect to find any shortcuts. Whatever time was needed to write them all down would be taken, neither more nor less. After all, what lay before him was joy and not suffering. Indeed, what can be more joyful than writing down beauty?

When he finally brought his work to a close, Mr. Plushal was considerably older than fifty-six. But this did nothing to lessen his feeling of satisfaction and fulfillment. On the contrary. How many people that old can say their lives have not been in vain, for they have collected beauty? Only one thing was left for him to do. There was room for just two more words at the bottom of the last page of the completely filled notebook. For the first time since he'd started his collection, he softened his handwriting a little. It was still austere, but also gentle, benevolent. Just the way a signature should be. Entering the notebook, he slowly pulled the back cover after him, as though lowering a heavy lid.

7. Stories

I TYPED THE LAST sentence of the story. But there was no time to sink into the unique feeling of relief brought by the completion of writing. Before I had managed to press two keys on the keyboard to save the file, the screen suddenly turned purple.

How awful! The monitor was indeed old, but I had nonetheless expected it to hold up for some time to come. Why did it have to go on the blink right then and spoil my moment of pleasure? What's more, the last thing I needed was an unforeseen expenditure.

Filled with frustration, I did something that actually made no sense. I turned off the monitor, waited a bit and then turned it on again. That's what people do who don't know anything about hardware, and I wasn't one of them. When things start going wrong, those not in the know first turn off everything they can. Whatever for? It might be their confusion, it might be to let off steam, or it might be the irrational hope that when they turn things back on, everything will be put magically back in place.

When the screen lit up again nothing, of course, was back in place. The purple shade was still there and at the bottom of the story, after a space of one line, something was written that hadn't been there a moment before. I bent down and looked at the short addendum:

Wonderful story! Congratulations!

Staring close up at the three words, I tried to figure out what was going on. The only thing that crossed my mind was that someone had linked up to my computer over the Internet and had been spying on me as I wrote. There is all manner of abuse over the Internet, but I had yet to hear of something similar. It would be truly terrible if such spying were possible. But that wasn't my main problem at the moment. Without even checking the lower right-hand corner of the screen I knew that the intruder hadn't come via the Internet because I wasn't online. Why should I be, anyway, when I was writing?

Bewilderment led me to repeat my senseless reaction. Even though I was aware that it wouldn't solve anything, I reached for the monitor button again. My hand remained in midair, however, because the cursor jumped down to the next line and started writing new text right before my eyes.

Turning the monitor off and on again won't get you anywhere.

I jumped back from the screen spontaneously, as though physically threatened. I felt the hair on the back of my neck stand on end. What was going on? How could he know what I intended to do? I started looking feverishly around my study, but a new message stopped me.

There isn't any camera, if that's what you're looking for.

Great restraint was needed to stop me from turning off the computer. If I did, though, I would lose the story, which hadn't been saved, and that had to be avoided at any cost. I brought my hands cautiously to the keyboard, as though it might bite me. I pressed two keys lightly, then quickly raised my fingers, but the normal confirmation that I'd saved the text was missing. In its place came a rapid series of letters in italics.

Everything is all right. The story is saved. Don't worry. We certainly couldn't let such a good story go to waste, could we?

I stared for some time at the four lines under the

last paragraph of the story. When I finally returned my hands to the keyboard, hesitating as before, I knew I was getting involved in something dodgy. But what choice did I have?

Who are you?

A collector of last stories.

There were much more important questions, of course, but all I did was type one word.

Last?

Yes. This is your last story. And probably your best. That is quite rare, by the way.

I paused briefly before my fingers touched the keyboard again.

Why would it be my last?

Isn't it obvious? Because you won't be writing any more.

This was completely crazy, but since I was already ambushed, I had to continue.

Why wouldn't I write any more? Who's going to prevent me?

You'll prevent yourself. At least I hope you will.

And why on earth would I do such a thing?

Because otherwise you'll die.

Irritation replaced my confusion. Nimble fingers typed angrily.

Listen here! I don't know how you're pulling this off and I really don't care. I've had enough. You've gone too far. I won't let anyone taunt me like that.

You haven't been to the doctor in a while, have you? It might be a good idea to find the time. How long are you going to pretend that the stitch at the base of your chest isn't getting worse?

I didn't answer right away. I brought a hand unconsciously to my chest.

How do you know? I haven't told anyone about it.

Is that important? You just confirmed it yourself.

I hoped it wasn't anything serious. I guess I'll have to go to the doctor.

The doctor won't be able to help you very much unless you help yourself.

By not writing?

That's right. Your very next story would be fatal. You would die of a heart attack just as you started to write it.

I thought of asking once again how he knew, but gave up. It really wasn't important.

And if I don't write anymore?

Then you will live to a rather ripe old age. The pains in your chest will disappear all by themselves. The doctor will give you a clean bill of health.

I thought it over a bit.

The choice, then, is between life without writing and writing that leads to death?

Yes. The choice is yours.

I hesitated briefly once again.

That's not much of a choice.

It isn't, but it's better than not having any choice at all.

Why do I deserve preferential treatment?

As I wrote the last word I knew what the answer would be.

Is that important?

What would happen if later on, when the doctor says I'm healthy, I started writing again?

You wouldn't get very far. Even the healthiest people can die a sudden death. There's no cheating with this. You have written your last story.

I sighed and pinched the bridge of my nose with thumb and index finger because a dull throb had started there.

Do you have a lot of last stories in your collection?

Yes. A lot.

Were their authors faced with this choice too?

They were.

What did they choose?

Most of them chose life. And longevity. Particularly since there is actually no alternative. There are some, how-

ever, who can't live without writing. They continue, even when they know what awaits them.

I can understand that.

Does that mean you'll join them?

I don't know. I have to think it over. It's not an easy decision to make.

It isn't, I agree. In any case, whatever you decide, I think you'll be happy to know that your last story is one of the nicest in my collection. I hope this brings you some consolation.

I laughed bitterly.

I feel better already.

Good. That's about all. I am honored to have had the chance to talk to a wonderful writer.

I'd already touched the keys, but there was no time to send an appropriate farewell. The text of our dialogue and the story that preceded it were suddenly highlighted in black, as when a block is marked, and then disappeared. The purple film went with it. The whiteness of the empty screen stared at me with blank eloquence.

I stared back at it, stock-still for a time. And then my fingers, already resting on the keyboard, seemed to start typing by themselves:

I typed the last sentence of the story. But there was no time to sink into the unique feeling of relief brought by the completion of writing. Before I had managed to press two keys on the keyboard to save the file, the screen suddenly turned purple.

I didn't have time to lower the cursor to a new paragraph. A sharp pain forced me to grab desperately at my chest.

8. Clippings

MR. POSPIHAL COLLECTED NEWSPAPER clippings. He'd been doing this since the age of sixty-two, when he retired. He'd spent his entire adult life working for the post office, rising from postman to manager. Working in the post office had taught him to respect order above all things. He was an innately orderly man, but the work at the post office had fully impressed on him the importance of averting *any* kind of disorder. Even deviating quite innocently from the rules or yielding however slightly to confusion could have unforeseeable consequences.

Maintaining order took time. Even before he'd become manager, Mr. Pospihal stayed at work longer than regulations required. Thorough preparations were needed before the workday began, and when it was over many things were left that needed attention. If he hadn't proceeded in such a way he would never have become manager. And promotion to that position didn't soften him a bit. Quite the contrary. He spent almost every waking hour at the post office, arriving considerably before the other employees and leaving long after them. It couldn't have been any other way. Before, he'd been responsible solely for himself, while as manager he was responsible for many other people.

Such commitment to his work didn't leave much time for a private life. Mr. Pospihal had never started a family, although he might have wanted one in his younger days. Later this desire diminished, and he even saw the merits of not being married and having children. He'd sacrificed himself for the greater good. It would have been hard to be a successful postal employee, let alone manager, if he'd been hampered by family obligations. The example of many of his colleagues confirmed this. Chiefly because they were family oriented, they did not do their jobs anywhere near as reliably and conscientiously as he did his.

When he retired, Mr. Pospihal had to face a double blow. First of all, he wasn't at all certain he'd left the post office in good hands. His opinion of the manager who succeeded him was far from good. No sooner had he taken up his position than he dropped the strict rules on employee behavior that Mr. Pospihal had unofficially introduced that dealt, for example, with how long the employees' hair and mustaches could be, and prohibited them from wearing short-sleeved shirts regardless of the temperature. He'd written the new manager a detailed letter, polite but severe, expressing his reasonable grounds for concern with regard to such indulgence, indicating the far-reaching consequences it might have. The lack of a reply even after a reasonable time had passed gave him great cause for concern and vexation.

The second blow fell even more heavily on Mr. Pospihal. Now retired, he had an abundance of the free time he'd consistently avoided while he was working. Since he didn't know how to fill his days, they were unbearably long in the beginning. And then he hit upon the best way to kill time. He would read the newspaper.

Mr. Pospihal used to read the newspaper before he retired, when he got home from work, but in a cursory fashion. He'd been reading the same serious daily newspaper from the capital ever since he was a young man, opening it after dinner before he went to bed. Fatigue, however, didn't allow him to get very engrossed. He'd leaf through the first section just enough to see the main headlines and might read an article from the front page if it seemed particularly important. Then sleep would steal over him. After all, he had to get up early in the morning.

Now he was finally able to read the newspaper at his leisure and when he wasn't sleepy. Right after breakfast he would settle into the only armchair in his small living room and stay there all the way till lunchtime, reading the paper from cover to cover. He didn't omit a thing, since he'd realized the meaning of being systematic long ago. Furthermore, the classified ads and obituaries were sometimes more interesting than front-page news.

Under such circumstances, it was inevitable that Mr. Pospihal would come across the section devoted to science published every Friday in the same place in the second half of the newspaper, after the section on culture and before the sports page. But the science section most likely would not have especially caught his eye if the very first article he read there hadn't been so exceptional. It was all about the fact that man is made of cosmic matter.

He didn't understand very much about science, although he certainly held it in great esteem. He'd been turned off science by complicated words he didn't know and even more complicated ideas he couldn't grasp. The author of this article, however, had taken great pains to write in simple language, and the idea itself, although unusual in every respect, could be understood with a certain amount of effort. In brief, it said just one place in the cosmos is the origin of almost all the atoms that make up living beings. That place is the core of very large suns. Humans, therefore, come from the stars.

Mr. Pospihal's previous opinion of himself, which was already good, was further reinforced by the knowledge of his cosmic origin. He cut the article out of the newspaper to keep it as a sort of genealogy and briefly toyed with the idea of framing it, then thought this would be going too far. He was content to put it in a transparent purple folder like those used in the post office to hold especially important documents. That way he could reread it whenever he wanted without damaging it by his touch or in any other way.

He waited impatiently for the following Friday to see whether the science section would repeat the same topic and was a bit disappointed when it was about something else. The new text attracted his attention nonetheless. After the very first reading he felt that he'd penetrated deep into the heart of the mysterious black holes. Everything was explained coherently, there was no confusion or ambiguity. He found a transparent purple folder for the second article too.

When Mr. Pospihal's collection had grown a bit, he finally realized what he liked so much about science. Order reigned. Unlike mankind's activities, where the inclination towards chaos was so evident, the world of science was perfectly ordered. Had he known this before he would have surely become a scientist and not a postal employee. Given his propensity for order, he would have gone quite far.

Who knows how long Mr. Pospihal would have enjoyed his collection and new focus in life, if it hadn't been for the one hundred and thirty-seventh article. What he read gave him such a shock that it shook the very foundations of his world. His heart started to pound and for a moment he was short of breath. Before mustering the courage to reread this text about the end of the universe he had to take a sedative.

The very author of the articles he'd been collecting so diligently and placing in transparent purple folders, the scientific commentator whose expertise and competence he trusted so much, had now put forward something altogether shocking and impossible. The universe, he claimed, would meet a terrible end. In one hundred twenty-five and a half billion years there would be no more galaxies or stars or planets. Or even people. There would be nothing but elementary particles wandering aimlessly and even they would finally disappear.

Once he'd calmed down a little, Mr. Pospihal wrote an angry letter to the newspaper's editor-in-chief, directly accusing him of irresponsibly publishing positively incorrect and highly disturbing information. Was that a way for the universe to end? How could such magnificent order end in supreme disorder? This was betraying the very essence of science!

Was the author of the article conscious of what he'd said? If what he said were true, what would be the point of making any effort, since everything was doomed from the outset? This, of course, could not and must not happen. Had he made a supreme effort his whole life through to keep the post office in impeccable shape just to have it finally turn into scattered atoms, and maybe not even that, regardless of how far in the future?

He expected an immediate reply from the editor-in-chief with the apology he was due. The immediate dismissal of the science commentator was taken for granted. Partial amends might be possible if they proposed that Mr. Pospihal write for the science section in the future. He already had the expertise and an oversight such as this would never afflict him. He knew all too well the meaning of order.

In the following days, the first thing Mr. Pospihal did was to check the newspaper's editorial page. Since the editor-in-chief's reply and apology were not forthcoming, he concluded that the editorial board was trying to hush up the scandal. Instead of making the whole affair public, they would send him a discreet letter and try to keep him quiet. First they would try persuasion, and if that didn't work they'd use bribery or even threats. But he wouldn't give in. Had it been something less important he might have turned a blind eye, but this was of the broadest cosmic proportions. He didn't have the right to retreat.

After several weeks had passed with still no letter, Mr. Pospihal concluded dejectedly that a great conspiracy was at work and, alas, he alone could do nothing against it. Disorder had triumphed over order, and all he could do was stand by helplessly and watch.

Overcome by frustration, the first thing he did was destroy his collection. As with everything else in his life, he did it systematically. He took a large pair of scissors, sharpened them a bit and then cut all the articles together with their purple folders into small pieces of the same size. And then, for the first time in his life, he did something unreasonable. He ate this plastic-coated confetti slowly and determinedly, even though the taste was quite abominable.

Then he sat in the armchair, prepared for what would follow. He was not surprised when he began soon to disintegrate. With perverse curiosity, as though this were happening to someone else and not himself, he watched himself dissolve. The connections that kept the atoms of his body together, what used to be cosmic matter, slowly started to break, and particles scattered chaotically about the living room. Soon, in one hundred billion years or so, they too would disappear forever.

9. Deaths

I WAS JUST ABOUT to fall asleep when a knock roused me. I opened my eyes and looked angrily towards the hospital room door. Who could that be now? Hadn't we agreed they wouldn't come until morning? A man has the right to die in peace, doesn't he? They were well aware of the fact that nothing more could be done, and as an experienced doctor, so was I. I had taken a strong sedative to fall asleep as soon as possible. Dying in my sleep was the very last favor I could do myself. Why were they taking it away from me now?

"Come in!" I said, as sharply as my general condition allowed.

The man who came in was tall and slender. He was wearing a long purple coat, its cheerfulness somewhat incongruous with his late middle age. A gray or olive-green shade would have been more suited to his thinning, salt-and-pepper hair and softly wrinkled face. But that, of course, was hardly important now.

"Good evening," he said and, without waiting for a reply, headed for the chair next to my pillow. He sat down, folded his hands in his lap and stared at me in silence. We stayed like that for a few moments, looking at each other.

I was the first to break the silence. "Don't you think it's rather late to visit a sick man?"

"It would indeed be late in just a few minutes. As it is, until you fall asleep, there's still time."

"Time for what? Who are you? How did you get into the hospital at this hour?"

"In what order would you like the answers? Let's start from the last question. It's the easiest. I was able to enter the hospital because no one stopped me."

"Wasn't the security officer on duty?"

"He was, but he didn't see me."

"How's that? Were you invisible or something?"

"You might say so."

I sighed. "Well, you don't look that way to me. What do you want?"

The visitor did not answer immediately. He again threw me a brief and silent look.

"Your death," he said at last in an even tone.

Now it was my turn to stare at him.

"Listen, I don't know who you are or how you got here. It makes no difference anyway. But unless you leave here at once, I'll call and have them throw you out."

"I suggest you do exactly that."

I hesitated a minute, then stretched out my hand and felt for the buzzer on the night table. I pushed it longer than was necessary. The nurse's rapid footsteps were heard coming down the hall.

I didn't say a word when she came in. It was enough to look at the chair next to the bed to understand why I'd called. But she came up to me as though we were alone in the room.

"How are you?" she asked gently.

I stared at her in confusion, not knowing what to say.

"I can't sleep," were the words that finally came out.

She patted the back of my hand.

"You'll fall asleep soon enough. Don't worry. You were given a strong dose."

Quite an effort was needed for me to give a fleeting smile.

"Thank you."

"I'm here if you need anything. All you have to do is ring."

"Thank you."

She returned my smile, straightened my covers a bit and then headed for the door. She stopped at it as though about to turn around, but didn't.

I waited for the nurse's footsteps to fade down the hall before I looked at the visitor again.

"Who are you?" I asked in a low voice.

"A death collector." His voice was still detached, as though saying something quite commonplace.

"Death collector?" I repeated rather foolishly.

"Yes. I collect deaths. It's not as unusual a hobby as it might seem. There are stranger ones. If you give me your death you will get something truly priceless in return."

"How can I give you my death?"

"It's easy. All you have to do is give your consent."

"That's all?"

"Yes."

"And then I won't die anymore?"

"You won't die."

"And I'll get something in return too?"

"By all means."

I paused for a moment.

"What?"

He too waited a bit before replying.

"If you had to choose the most beautiful day of your life, which one would it be?"

"That's a difficult question. I'd have to think it over."

"You don't have much time for that. There must be one day you remember as being exceptional. A day when you were especially happy."

"There were days like that, of course. But why are they important now? They're gone forever."

"One could come back."

"How?"

"I could give you an explanation but it would take some time and the sedative will knock you out any moment. We have to be quick."

"In what way would it come back? I don't understand."

"In such a way that you would be in that day again. You would live through it exactly the same way you did the first time. You wouldn't know anything about your life to come. As though it never happened."

I thought it over briefly.

"And at the end of that day? Is that when I would die?"

"No. You would never die. Your death would be in my collection."

"Would I continue to live out the rest of my life?"

"No, you wouldn't. You would go back to your most beautiful day. You would relive it over and over, every day. Forever. So, do you agree to exchange your death for such an eternity?"

The sedative was starting to take effect. Considerable effort was needed to keep my eyes open.

"Why wouldn't I agree? Anyone in my place would say yes."

The visitor smiled broadly.

"Wonderful!" he said in a voice that was no longer indifferent. "That means we have a deal."

"It's a deal," I confirmed in a soft voice, eyes half-closed.

The smile stayed on his face a short while longer, but when he spoke again his voice had become detached like before.

"Not everyone accepts my offer, you know."

"Who would choose death when he's offered eternity, especially one filled with a beautiful day?" I asked almost in a whisper, finally closing my eyes.

His answer seemed to come from a distance. "Eternity lasts a very long time, even when it's ideal. I hope you'll enjoy it nonetheless."

A wave of fear suddenly coursed through my fading consciousness. I vaguely suspected that something wasn't right, but couldn't figure out what it was. And then it didn't matter anymore. I started to wake up, filled with unexpected joy. Something very nice awaited me in the coming day.

10. Emails

MR. PAVEK COLLECTED EMAILS. He'd been doing this since he retired at age sixty-five. He hadn't been able to do it before because he hadn't had a computer at home. When he finally left the State Archive after four decades of dedicated service, he was given the computer he'd used for the last thirteen and a half years as a token of recognition. The satisfaction he received from this gift was not marred by the knowledge that it was to be written off as obsolete since new computers were on the way.

Had they given him a new computer, it would have brought him nothing but trouble, since he was unable to cope with any but his old one. He was used to it, although that had taken some doing. He'd needed considerably more time than the other employees to master a mischievous and unpredictable machine that seemed determined never to do what he wanted it to.

He'd gone through countless traumatic experiences during training. All his efforts were ruined by clumsiness and blunders: once he'd caused a fire and another time an ambulance was called because he'd had a nervous breakdown. But finally, after a little more than two years and two months, he could proudly say that he'd subjugated the computer at long last, at least as far as the basic archive program was concerned.

His colleagues used many other programs that often had nothing to do with work, but it never crossed his mind to do something similar. If anyone had asked why, he would have answered that he definitely did not approve of such an abuse of working hours and state-owned equipment, but since no one ever did ask, there was no need for self-delusion. He avoided other programs because they frightened him.

When he brought the computer home, fear came along with it. Since he now had nothing to do with the only program he was skilled at, he would have to learn new programs, i.e. go through the trauma all over again. He could, indeed, have avoided this by not using the computer at all. That's what he did at first. He put the housing and monitor in a corner and covered them with a purple flannel cloth. This soon seemed like an unnecessary waste, so he finally reconciled himself to the inevitable.

His first dilemma was which program to choose. Different computer games favored by his former colleagues were out of the question. He couldn't imagine wasting time so irresponsibly, even in retirement. The best thing would be to do something useful. But what? Lots of people use a computer like a typewriter, but what would he write?

Who knows how long he would have spent pondering what to do with his computer if he hadn't seen an advertisement in the newspaper lauding the benefits of the Internet, particularly if you were looking for a job. Mr. Pavek knew that the Internet was quite widespread and that people enthused over it, but he'd avoided it out of the same fear that prevented him from trying new programs. Now, however, he had no way out. He would have to overcome that fear.

A pleasant surprise awaited him: it turned out that using the Internet was not as difficult as he'd feared. There was no nervous breakdown and not even any lasting trauma. Twice he thought he'd backed himself into a corner, but he quickly got out of it by carefully following the clear instructions. Everything was set for simple and easy use.

Hooking up to the Internet was just like opening a big window onto a vast world that included many different possibilities. It soon became apparent that Mr. Pavek wouldn't have to look for something to occupy his time. Work came looking for him.

The very same day he hooked up to the Internet he started to receive emails. Even though he didn't know the senders and had no idea how they'd found his address, he was pleased nonetheless. Hardly anyone ever wrote to Mr. Pavek, and now whenever he looked at his virtual mailbox there were always a few letters waiting.

His mail consisted of various offers that didn't interest him very much. Those that made him blush were the most numerous. Indeed, how could anyone think that he, at his age, might need to lengthen certain organs or use products that brought fierce and long-lasting ecstasy? But he didn't get mad at those who sent the offers because their intentions were undoubtedly noble. How could you blame people who were trying to fill your life with pleasure, regardless of the fact that it was impossible?

As soon as Mr. Pavek read his first message, his archivist's instincts went to work. He knew quite well what happened to documents that were not quickly logged as prescribed. This was the basic principle of his profession. Things get lost in an instant and disappear without a trace unless they are filed properly. And one never knows how valuable they might be. Didn't it often happen that papers everyone considered inconsequential had turned out to be of great importance? Many people failed to realize that a proper archive was the foundation of every ordered society.

He adjusted his archive program slightly so he could store emails. Every message was first given a file number and classification. The abbreviation system he used at work came in quite handy. Instead of writing "erotic offer", which would make him feel awkward whenever he saw it, it was enough to put "er.ofr." This had a respectable and professional look to it.

Once the message was logged, he had to answer it. Good manners so required. What would the people who wrote think about him if he didn't reply? Remarks might be made about Mr. Pavek—that he was excessively fastidious, rather unsociable, too much a creature of habit—but certainly not that he was impolite.

His replies were short and official, as befitted correspondence with people he didn't know personally. He didn't go into a lengthy explanation as to why he wasn't interested in what had been offered. He thanked them for the offer, allowed for the possibility that he might change his mind in the future should his circumstances alter, and ended with a formal greeting. Everything in proper measure.

Although Mr. Pavek didn't see the connection, with every reply he sent he received more and more new offers. Barely two weeks after he'd hooked up to the Internet he was overwhelmed with work. His virtual mailbox never seemed to be empty and he spent an increasing amount of time logging his emails and answering them.

His replies sped up considerably when he remembered that he didn't have to compose a new email every time. While still at work he'd learned one of the facilities that computers provide. He'd had no use for it before, but now it proved quite convenient. Once a text was written it could easily be copied to another place, and his answers were always more or less the same anyway. He didn't do this mechanically, however. He would always introduce a small change, just enough to keep his conscience clear. He didn't want it to seem that he was merely skimming through his work. Something small would set each message apart: the word order, an added or missing adjective, the location of the signature.

His speedy replies only brought momentary relief because the influx of emails soon turned into an avalanche. While still employed, Mr. Pavek would occasionally encounter a large workload where great effort was required and he had to stay over-time. But that couldn't be compared with what was now pouring down on him. Hundreds of new mails gushed out of his virtual mailbox whenever he opened it.

This correspondence was no great hardship, however, because otherwise Mr. Pavek wouldn't have known how to pass the time. He didn't know how to be idle. He now spent almost all his waking time at the computer and had even reduced his sleep to only four and a half hours, but if that was the price he had to pay to fill his life with something, then he had no choice. The question as to whether the work had any meaning didn't bother him, just as it hadn't when he worked at the State Archive. Only uneducated and ignorant people needed to have the meaning of archiving explained to them; it was clear and obvious to those with any intelligence.

Although he could be unrelenting with regard to himself, forcing himself to work beyond all customary measure, the computer required due consideration. Unlike him, this device had physical limits. Three months and seventeen days after he'd started to log emails his hard disk was finally filled up. If he'd been given a new computer when he retired this problem would not have appeared quite so quickly, but the old hard disk had a very modest capacity.

Mr. Pavek was in a bind with no easy way out. Had his pension been larger, he could have bought a new hard disk, but he could barely make ends meet as it was. Unplanned expenditures were out of the question. And the virtual mailbox was getting fuller all the time.

He stared helplessly at the screen with its flickering warning in large letters: HARD DISK FULL! Something had to be done urgently, but he didn't know what. But just when panic was getting the upper hand, something happened. The warning suddenly disappeared and was replaced with his image, as though the screen were a mirror. But the reflection was not faithful, for Mr. Pavek's virtual face was deformed by a scream. It was soundless, because the old computer didn't have speakers. This made no difference anyway, as there was no one to hear it. The chair in front of the screen was empty.

11. Hopes

I HEARD THE DOOR open and then footsteps headed my way. Even though I couldn't see anything, my head turned in reflex towards whomever was approaching, giving my neck a bit of a crick. The kidnapper stopped next to me. Nothing happened for several tense moments, and then he took off my hood.

I squinted after spending so much time in the dark, even though the light wasn't very strong. I looked around, taking in my surroundings. I'd had no idea where I was, but for some reason I'd thought I was in some sort of windowless, sparsely furnished cellar. I could tell that I was sitting in an armchair, tied with handcuffs to the wooden armrests, and this had confused me. Such comfort was incongruous with a bare, subterranean cell.

One look was enough to realize that my suspicions were wrong. The armchair stood in the middle of a spacious and high-ceilinged study. All four walls were lined with shelves containing heavy volumes. There were only two interruptions to this uniform background. A padded door broke the wall of books to my left, while the opposite wall was divided in two by a window that reached almost to the ceiling. It was covered with heavy purple drapes.

Right above my head was a chandelier, but it was not switched on. The only source of light was a shaded lamp on the solid wood desk in front of me. Along with it were a pitcher of water, a glass and a small hourglass.

On the other side of the table rose the arched back of a deeply engraved black chair.

I'd been wrong in one other respect too. I'd been convinced that my kidnapper was a young, thickset male. True, he'd never spoken, so his voice had never confirmed this assumption, but it had somehow seemed natural. The person now standing before me was much more reminiscent of a retired literature professor than of a hardened kidnapper.

He had to be in his sixties, with thinning gray hair, and was slight of build. He was wearing a long bathrobe of the same purple color as the drapes. Small round reading glasses dangled on a chain around his neck.

"Hello," he said, smiling.

"Hello," I replied, after hesitating briefly, feeling this was a ridiculous way to start a conversation between kidnapper and kidnapped.

He indicated the handcuffs. "I'm sorry for the inconvenience. I believe you understand they are necessary for the moment. I hope they don't bother you too much. How do you feel? Is there anything you want?"

I hesitated again, keeping my eyes on him. "I'd like a sip of water. I'm thirsty."

He nodded. "Of course."

He went to the desk and poured some water into the glass. He brought it up to my mouth and tipped it. As I drank, water dribbled down my chin.

"Excuse me." He quickly took a matching handkerchief out of the bathrobe pocket and wiped my face. Then he went back to the desk, put the glass down, walked around to the other side and sat in the chair. His head dipped below the top of the chair back. He inverted the hourglass. The sand in the upper chamber started to seep into the lower chamber.

We looked at each other for several moments in silence.

"What do you want from me?" I said, breaking the stalemate. "If it's money you want, a real bundle, then you've kidnapped the wrong person. No one will pay to get me back."

"I'm not looking for a bundle of money."

"Then what are you looking for?"

"Some things are more valuable than money."

"Sure they are, but kidnappers couldn't care less."

"There are kidnappers and kidnappers. Let me ask you a question in return. What price would you be willing to pay to be free once again?"

I'd never been kidnapped before, but even so I hadn't expected negotiations with a kidnapper could be anything like this.

"I wouldn't know. If it's not about money, what else do I have that could possibly interest you?"

"There certainly is something, otherwise you wouldn't be here. But let's turn the question around. What would you be unwilling to give in exchange for freedom?"

I fixed my eyes on the old man. Had I not been bound to an armchair, I might have found this strange conversation in an even stranger place interesting, in a rather twisted way.

"I don't know," I said in all sincerity. "I'd have to think it over. It's not an easy question."

"It's not, I agree. But I'm afraid we don't have much time." He indicated the hourglass in front of me, its gray stream flowing steadily, as though this explained everything. "I'd like to help, if you consent. Would you abandon all hope if that would bring you freedom?"

"Hope?" I repeated, bewildered. "What hope?"

"Hope in general. The right to hope for anything in life."

"I don't understand. How could I abandon hope?"

"Easily. Just by saying so."

Then it hit me. This wasn't an ordinary kidnapper.

I'd been kidnapped by one of those demented types who are in the grip of deranged ideas. Looks can be quite deceptive. The polished elderly man sitting in front of me was the last person in the world I would have thought had lost his mind. I had to be very careful. He might be crazy, but he certainly wasn't stupid.

"So, it's enough to say that I abandon all hope," I said in a low voice, "and you will release me?" I raised my hands a little, making the handcuffs rattle.

"That's right," he replied with a smile.

"There aren't any other conditions?"

"No."

I sighed. "All right, then I abandon all hope," I said formally.

The old man's smile broadened. "Very good! I am very happy things went so smoothly with you."

He stood up, took the hourglass and placed it horizontally.

"Sometimes it can be quite unpleasant," he continued after going around the table and stopping in front of me. "Some people prefer hope to freedom. They feel they can live without freedom, but not without hope."

I was briefly tempted to ask him what had happened to them, but concluded that it was actually none of my concern. Everyone has the right to their preferences. But there was one thing I had to know.

"If it's not a secret, would you mind telling me what you get out of the fact that people abandon all hope?"

"It's no secret. I am a hope collector."

He was as laconic as when he'd mentioned the hourglass. Indeed, why explain something when it's as clear as day?

"Oh, that's it," I said, as though grasping a simple truth.

The old man picked up the hood from the back of the chair.

"I'm afraid I'll have to put it on you again. Discretion is very important in this business. You do understand, don't you?"

"Of course," I agreed from underneath the hood.

"You can take it off in about fifteen minutes. And you won't be handcuffed anymore. You will be completely free once again. Please don't reproach me too much for anything unpleasant you may have experienced. Unfortunately it could not be helped."

"Reproach you for what? It wasn't the least bit unpleasant. Quite the contrary."

When I took off the hood fifteen minutes later, squinting wasn't enough. I had to close my eyes, blinded by the bright sunlight. As soon as I opened them again, however, I knew at once that something wasn't right. I should have been overjoyed at getting my freedom back without paying anything. But all I felt was a deep sense of hopelessness.

12. Collections

MR. POKORNI COLLECTED COLLECTIONS. He'd been doing this his whole life. He had neither the time nor the patience to put them together himself, so he got them ready-made. He was rich enough to pay however much it took if he found a collection to his liking. In spite of this, suspicions were raised periodically regarding how he'd come by some of his collections. Rumors were spread that he stole them, that he used blackmail, and that he would not shrink from murder just to get what he wanted. Once an investigation was conducted into the origin of one of the collections, but nothing illegal was ever proven.

He was very secretive about his collections. He did not deny that he had a rich collection of collections, but he refused to give out any details. In the normal course of things they would have remained outside the public eye, if it weren't for yours truly, the omniscient storyteller, from whom nothing can be hidden. Or almost nothing, as it turns out.

Given my privileged position as omniscient storyteller, the first thing to disclose is where Mr. Pokorni kept his collections. In view of his wealth and the value of the collections, one might expect him to have kept them in a special room, perhaps an armor-plated underground chamber protected by all-powerful electronic devices and guards who were armed to the teeth.

Nothing, however, could be farther from the truth. Mr. Pokorni kept his collections in a small side room.

It had previously been storage space for things that were rarely used. Then these things were thrown out and two gray metal shelves were installed on the walls, facing each other to the left and right of the door. The shelves stretched the whole length of the walls, from floor to ceiling, and each one had twelve partitions.

The small room would have had normal illumination if one of the collections hadn't needed purple lighting, as a result of which the bare light bulb hanging from a long wire was purple. The uninitiated will probably be most surprised by the fact that the collection storage room was not locked. All those with access to Mr. Pokorni's house could enter it without a second thought. This rarely happened, though, and even the owner went there infrequently. The most habitual visitors were the servants who went in to dust the collections every Wednesday morning, although there was hardly anything to dust.

At first glance it might seem that Mr. Pokorni had put his collections on the shelves at random. They did indeed look disorganized, as though put there only temporarily until a better place was found for them. This, however, was a mere illusion. Their owner knew exactly where each of the collections was located, although he might have had trouble explaining the criteria he'd used to place them there. Luckily, he didn't have to answer to anyone for his actions.

At the risk of an oversimplified explanation of this division, offered by your omniscient storyteller, and one that Mr. Pokorni might not agree with, it might be said that the left-hand shelves contained tangible collections while the right-hand shelves held collections with less substance.

A complete list of the collections naturally cannot be given here, because otherwise this story would turn into a catalogue, which would not be advisable. It is useful nevertheless to mention the most important ones, in order to add charm to the story. For example, one whole section on the left side was covered with cardboard boxes containing silver-plated cigarette cases filled with someone's nail clippings. There was also a notebook with the autographs of people who'd had the misfortune to die not long after they had signed it. Then there was an album to which an ardent collector had been adding pictures of himself for decades. Another interesting specimen was a notebook with words written in it that someone had found particularly beautiful. There was a remarkable collection of plastic folders containing newspaper clippings on scientific topics, and there was a computer hard disk filled with neatly filed emails.

While the left side featured a confusion of sizes and forms, the opposite side possessed a sort of uniformity, although here as well, had anyone been so inclined, quite a lot could have been done to improve the order, particularly the disposition of colors. The right side resembled a pharmacy, since it contained nothing but vials. They were all round with glass stoppers, and the only thing that differentiated them was their hue, resulting in a multicolored dissonance.

There was no way of telling what each little bottle contained. Mr. Pokorni had not put labels on them or denoted their contents in any other way, because this was unnecessary. He knew exactly what was in the bottles he'd collected. If it weren't for your omniscient storyteller, all this would have remained an absolute secret, but here is a chance to shed at least a bit of light on it.

The purple vials that required lighting of the same color and were the most numerous contained days of the pasts of people with a sweet tooth. The dark green ones were filled to the brim with a special type of dream. The bright yellow ones were the repository of the airy material that last stories are made of. The black ones, quite appropriately, received deaths, while the colorless ones, seemingly quite ordinary, were the home of hopes.

Who knows how long this collection of collections would have languished in the storeroom had the shelves been able to receive an infinite number of new collections. But even though they were large, they were not without limit and so one Thursday morning the inevitable happened. Mr. Pokorni came with a new collection and he had no place to put it. He tried to make room by shifting around the older collections, but to no avail.

This, of course, was not a serious problem, particularly not for someone as wealthy as Mr. Pokorni. He had several solutions at his disposal. The simplest would have been to put a new shelf on the third wall facing the door, currently unused. If this had not been to his liking for some reason, he could have moved the collections to a larger room. He certainly had plenty of them. He could even have set aside one whole house for his collections.

But he did not resort to any of these possibilities. When it became clear that there was no room for the new collection on either of the shelves, Mr. Pokorni put it on the floor and left the room. He soon returned with a large wicker basket. What follows is not recommended reading for overly sensitive or highly strung individuals.

As though these were worthless old things and not priceless objects, Mr. Pokorni started on the left-hand shelves and put the collections into the basket. He threw them in without the slightest concern that they might be damaged. Periodic sounds of breakage did nothing to slow him down or deter him. When he had filled the basket, he took it to the lighted fireplace in the large drawing room. He emptied its contents onto the floor then went back to the storeroom. After bringing four more baskets full, he drew a large leather armchair up to the fireplace, sat in it and got down to work.

It took hours to burn the tangible collections. Mr. Pokorni would wait patiently for one collection to burn completely before he threw a new one into the flames. Whatever wouldn't burn was returned to the basket to be thrown into the garbage. As he watched the flames engulf objects that others had lovingly collected for years, his face showed not the slightest emotion. It was as expressionless as if he were doing a daily chore.

When the time came for the right-hand shelves, he had to be more careful. He didn't throw the vials into the basket but placed them in an orderly fashion, making sure they didn't break. Instead of taking the basket to the fireplace, he took it to a large terrace overlooking lush gardens of evergreens. He brought five full baskets of bottles and placed them around a deckchair covered in purple canvas.

Dusk had already settled when he sat in the deckchair and started to open the vials. He paid no attention to the order in which he did this and was soon swathed in a mixture of floral fragrances. Days, as one might suspect, smelled of violets, dreams smelled of lilacs, stories of roses, death, contrary to all expectations, smelled of gardenias, and hopes of hyacinths. There was a multitude of other fragrances as well, heavy and light, penetrating and barely perceptible. They swirled around Mr. Pokorni invisibly for some time and then scattered about the gardens, making them briefly more fragrant than usual.

After the insubstantial contents had been released from the last bottle and the multitude of glass containers like so many empty shells had been taken to the garbage dump, one might pause to wonder why Mr. Pokorni had acted this way. This question, unfortunately, must remain unanswered. Even your omniscient storyteller is not powerful enough to peer into the head of this rich collector. Perhaps this is for the best. What would be the point in finding out why he destroyed the collections? It certainly would not bring them back.

Contributors

About the author

Zoran Živković was born in Belgrade, Serbia, on October 5, 1948. Until his recent retirement, he was a full professor at the Faculty of Philology, the University of Belgrade, teaching creative writing. He is one of the most translated contemporary Serbian writers: by the end of 2019 there were more than 100 foreign editions of his books of fiction, published in 23 countries, in 20 languages.

Živković has won several literary awards for his fiction, beginning with the Miloš Crnjanski award in 1994 for his novel *The Fourth Circle*. In 2003, Živković's mosaic novel *The Library* won a World Fantasy Award for Best Novella; in 2007 his novel *The Bridge* won the Isidora Sekulić award; and in 2007 he received the Stefan Mitrov Ljubiša award for lifetime achievement in literature. In 2014 and 2015 he received three awards for his contribution to the literature of fantastika: Art-Anima, Stanislav Lem and The Golden Dragon.

Zoran Živković has been recognized with his selection as European Grand Master for 2017 by the European Science Fiction Society at the 39th Eurocon in Dortmund, Germany.

Živković is the author of the 22 books of fiction:

The Fourth Circle (1993)
Time Gifts (1997)
The Writer (1998)
The Book (1999)
Impossible Encounters (2000)
Seven Touches of Music (2001)
The Library (2002)
Steps through the Mist (2003)
Hidden Camera (2003)
Compartments (2004)
Four Stories till the End (2004)
Twelve Collections and the Teashop (2005)
The Bridge (2006)
Miss Tamara, The Reader (2006),
Amarcord (2007)
The Last Book (2007)
Escher's Loops (2008)
The Ghostwriter (2009)
The Five Wonders of the Danube (2011)
The Grand Manuscript (2012)
The Compendium of the Dead (2015)
The Image Interpreter (2016)

About the artist

Youchan Ito was born 1968 in Aichi prefecture, Japan. She launched her career as a graphic designer in 1988, becoming a freelancer illustrator in 1991 and founding Togoru Co., Ltd. with her husband in 2000. In 2017 the company was reborn as Togoru Art Works. She works with a wide range of genres including cover art and design for science fiction, mysteries and horror titles, as well as illustrations for children's books.
www.youchan.com

www.ingramcontent.com/pod-product-compliance
Lightning Source LLC
Chambersburg PA
CBHW030356180626
46812CB00007B/2910